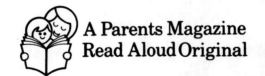

A Parents Magazine
Read Aloud Original

The Clown-Arounds Have a Party

Library of Congress Cataloging in Publication Data.
Cole, Joanna. The clown-arounds have a party.
SUMMARY: The funniest family in town pull some
of their best high jinks to cheer up homesick Cousin Fizzy.
[1. Clowns—Fiction.   2. Homesickness—Fiction.]
I. Smath, Jerry, ill.   II. Title.
PZ7.C67346Cm   [E]   82-2128
ISBN 0-8193-1085-9   AACR2
ISBN 0-8193-1086-7   (lib. bdg.)

The Clown-Arounds Have a Party

by **Joanna Cole**   pictures by **Jerry Smath**

Parents Magazine Press
New York

To my brothers, Joe, John,
and Jim (Krenshaw) Smath—J.S.

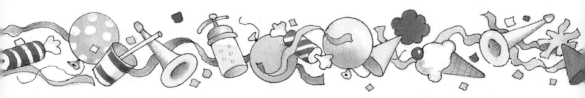

Do you know the Clown-Arounds?
They're the funniest family in town.

There's Mrs. Clown-Around,
Mr. Clown-Around,
their daughter, Bubbles,
the Baby,
and Wag-Around, their dog.

Everything about the Clown-Arounds
is funny.

Their dinner plates,

their lamp,

their rug,

even their refrigerator!

But nothing is as funny as
the Clown-Arounds themselves.
They are always playing tricks
on each other.

They like to tell jokes and riddles.

And they love to act silly.
Uh-oh. It's silly time again
at the Clown-Arounds' house.

One weekend, Cousin Fizzy came
to visit the Clown-Arounds.
They gave him a big hello.
Bubbles gave him a hand
with his suitcase, too.

The Clown-Arounds invited Fizzy
to come in and sit down.
Everyone was having a good time . . .

But then Fizzy started feeling homesick.

So Bubbles tried extra hard
to show Fizzy a good time.

Baby offered Fizzy a special treat.

Even Wag-Around
tried to help.

But nothing worked.
Fizzy still felt homesick,
so he went to take a nap.

Then Bubbles
got an idea.

While Fizzy was asleep,
the Clown-Arounds hopped into their car.
They almost got lost . . .

But finally they found the right place.
They got a big welcome.

Then they packed up their car
and started home.

They got back in the nick of time.
Fizzy was just waking up.

Now he had no reason to be homesick.

So Fizzy joined the fun.

The Clown-Arounds think that the
best way to spend a weekend
is to have a house party.
Don't you?

About the Author

JOANNA COLE enjoys writing the story
and inventing the jokes that will appear in
the pictures of the Clown-Arounds books.
"But Jerry Smath's illustrations are still a
surprise," says Ms. Cole. "He always comes
up with something I didn't think of. That's
the fun and privilege of working with a
terrific artist."

Joanna Cole was an elementary school
teacher and a children's book editor before
she turned to writing full time. She writes
both fiction and nonfiction for children,
magazine articles, and is now working on
a nonfiction book for grown-ups.

Ms. Cole lives with her husband and
daughter in New York City.

About the Artist

JERRY SMATH does free-lance illustration for magazines and children's school books. He wrote and illustrated two books for Parents, *BUT NO ELEPHANTS* and *THE HOUSEKEEPER'S DOG*. He also illustrated *THE CLOWN-AROUNDS* by Joanna Cole. "When I work with an author," says Mr. Smath, "we must both think and feel like children for the book to turn out right!"

Mr. Smath and his wife, Valerie, a graphic designer, live in Westchester County, New York.